MY LAST MARTINI

MARTINI

S T O R I E S

OTHER BOOKS BY BARRY GIFFORD

MY LAST MARTINI

S T O R I E S

BARRY GIFFORD

CRANE HILL
PUBLISHERS

Library of Congress Cataloging-In-Publication Data

Gifford, Barry, 1946–

   My last martini / Barry Gifford.

     p. cm.

   Contents: My last martini—New mysteries of Paris—The Tunisian
notebook—The brief confession of an unrepentant erotic—The yellow
palace—The old days—A fair price.

  ISBN 1-57587-136-X

   L. Title

PS3557.I283 M9 2000

813'.54—dc21

00–027682

Acknowledgments

"My Last Martini" appeared, in different form, in the *San Francisco
Chronicle.* "The Tunisian Notebook" originally appeared in *The Berkeley
Monthly* and *The Boston Monthly.* "New Mysteries of Paris" appeared,
in different form, under the title "Nadja" in *Zyzzyva* (San Francisco).
"The Old Days" appeared in *Max (Milan).* "A Fair Price" appeared in
San Francisco.

The author wishes to thank Russell Chatham and Clark City Press
for permission to reprint the stories that were published in the book
New Mysteries of Paris (1991).

To Gino & Diep

CONTENTS

MY LAST MARTINI

The bar of the Hotel Luneau in Paris is a popular meeting place, especially in the late afternoon and early evening. There is a rather ordinary walnut bar with eight stools and brass footrest, but the charming features of the place are the seven maroon leather banquettes that form a half-circle facing the bar, and the three Marie Antoinette chandeliers with dim plum bulbs that convey the impression of a first-class cruise ship's lounge. The atmosphere is, therefore, both convivial and intimate. Patrons sit alone, reading, smoking, or merely gazing around; occasionally there are groups of three or four, but most common are the couples: The Luneau bar is a favorite rendezvous of lovers.

It was there that I was recently told a remarkable story by a complete stranger, a woman I had never seen before nor expect to see again, except by chance. I had met my friend Sharif, as I do most every Wednesday evening at about six-thirty when we're both in town. Sharif is a businessman in his mid-sixties, his businesses being oil and real estate. He keeps apartments in Paris and Houston, and a house in Algiers that is, apparently, quite palatial. I can't say for certain since I've never been to Algiers, though Sharif has invited me a dozen times to visit. Sharif thinks I don't accept his invitations because I'm afraid the fundamentalist terrorists might slit my throat. Seeing as how I am a white, beardless male, I cannot discount this as a possibility, but the real truth is that I just plain hate to travel.

On this particular evening, Sharif had an early dinner date with another friend, so we spent perhaps forty-five minutes together, during which time we each consumed two martinis and a plate of olives. I believe our conversation concerned the American government's policy of limiting individual com-panies' investment in Iranian oil to twenty million dollars, and the benefits this has bestowed upon other countries; and the upcoming Prix de l'Arc de Triomphe. Sharif thought the Americans' approach to Iran impossibly parochial, and predicted that Hélissio would take the Arc. I could not dispute him on the oil issue, but I felt that Peintre Célèbre, the American horse, stood a hell of a chance.

After Sharif had gone, I sat quietly, surveying the scene, savoring the dregs of my second martini. Two martinis don't ordinarily affect me other than to provide a feeling of false elation that I treasure for the thirty or so minutes it lasts. I rarely exceed my usual limit of two, however; an excess of elation, I've found, puts the world around me in a light so unflattering that I've been tempted once or twice to make an attempt at extinguishing it. For some reason, when the waiter came by to collect the tab, I astonished myself by ordering a third. The waiter nodded and headed back to the bar.

"Do you mind if I join you?" The voice came from an occupant of the booth to my left.

I looked over and saw an attractive dark-haired woman in her mid-thirties. She was holding a half-filled martini glass in her right hand.

"I heard you order a martini," she said, "and I thought you might be someone I could talk to."

By the time she'd finished this sentence, the woman had slid out of her booth and taken the place of Sharif in mine.

"By all means," I responded.

I studied her as closely as was possible in the muted light. She was even better looking than I first thought. She wore her chestnut hair up, with modest bangs. Her eyes were the same color as her hair. Only her teeth were imperfect, deeply stained by tobacco. She did not, however, light a cigarette while we were together. The waiter arrived with my martini.

"Would you like another?" I asked.

"Thank you, I would."

I passed this information along to the waiter and he went away. I was impressed that she did not feel the need to guzzle the remainder of the drink she kept in her hand, at which I inadvertently glanced.

"You're a martini man," she said, "you know they're not to be rushed."

I settled back and watched her take a sip. The toothpick and olive were still in the glass. She didn't say anything else until after the waiter had come and gone again, leaving a fresh martini in front of her. She smiled at me. Her teeth were almost red. Now she downed the last of the martini she'd brought with her, punctuating it by sliding the impaled olive off the toothpick using only the tip of her tongue. In the peculiar light of the Luneau bar, the hue of her tongue matched that of her teeth. She chewed the olive with her eyes closed, then dropped the toothpick back into the glass.

When she'd finished off the olive, she reopened her eyes and said, "Two is my limit. Martinis, that is, not olives."

She pointed with a black fingernail to the drink awaiting her.

"This," she said, with a puma's smile, "will be my third."

I nodded at the glass in front of me.

"Mine, too."

She picked hers up and held it out toward me. I did likewise.

"*Santé,*" she said.

"*Santé,*" I repeated.

We sipped. Remarkably, mine was still very cold.

"Are you Italian?" I asked, though we were speaking French.

"My mother is from Roma."

"And your father?"

"From the country. But he was not pure Italian. He was half-Polish."

"Dead?"

"Yes."

"I'm sure you favor your mother."

She smiled again but quickly cut it off.

"Look," she said, "you must think I'm a bit forward, if not crazy. But I want you to know, I'm not a working girl."

"It wouldn't matter to me if you were, since I'm not at present in the market."

"So. I said I thought you were someone I could talk to. I hope you are, because I have a story I'd like to tell."

"I'm in no particular hurry," I said. "It's a slow night."

"Good. My grandmother, my father's mother, had eight children, six boys and two girls. My father was the third oldest. When she married, she was sixteen years old, a virgin. She lived in a small village in Tuscany. The man to whom she was given in marriage by her parents could not make love. This, of course, she had not known before the marriage."

"Was it annulled?"

"No, impossible. In my grandmother's village, a marriage was forever."

She took a long sip of her martini. I did the same with mine.

"My grandmother was very upset by this, since she wanted to have many children."

"I can barely imagine," I said.

"She made her husband, who was a farmer, ask his Polish worker, who lived in a room underneath the house, below ground, to make love to her. It was this Pole who was the father of my father and his five brothers and two sisters."

"Who knew beside your grandmother and her husband and the Pole?"

"Nobody, until many years later. The Pole would take a broomstick and poke the end of the handle against the ceiling of his underground room to let my grandmother know when he wanted to make love to her."

I swallowed half of what was left of my martini.

"What a remarkable circumstance," I said.

"My father found out when he was twenty-two years old, after my grandmother's husband had died."

"Your grandmother told him?"

"Yes. It was accidental, perhaps. He had done something she didn't like and she cursed him, calling him a dumb Polish bastard. Of course she'd cursed him many times before, but she'd never called him a dumb Polish bastard, and he asked her why she'd said that particular thing."

"And she confessed."

"Yes, it all came out. She cried bitterly and told my father how she had hated both her husband and his Polish worker. She did it to have a family, but finally one night when the Pole banged his broom handle against her floor, she refused to answer. The next morning, when her husband was ready to work, the Pole was gone. He disappeared and nobody in the family ever saw him again."

"How did this news affect your father and the others?"

"My father left for Roma the same day. He rarely saw his mother after that. It was my mother who took me and my sister and brother to see our grandmother. My father was a terrible womanizer, going from girl to girl always. My mother was quite an unhappy woman."

"But she stayed with your father."

"Until two years before he died. Then he was living with another woman."

Both of us finished our drinks. The woman suddenly leaned over and kissed me full on the lips, a cold martini kiss.

"I'm glad I was right," she said.

"About?"

"Your being a good listener. Often when I have the need to talk, it's difficult to find someone, and I've no use for the church."

She withdrew from the booth, stood for a moment looking at me, then walked away. The waiter came over.

"Another martini, sir?" he asked.

"No," I said, pointing to my empty glass, "this one was definitely my last."

NEW MYSTERIES
OF PARIS

I was recently told a story that was so stupid, so melancholy, and so moving: a man comes into a hotel one day and asks to rent a room. He is shown up to number 35. As he comes down a few minutes later and leaves the key at the desk, he says: "Excuse me, I have no memory at all. If you please, each time I come in, I'll tell you my name: Monsieur Delouit. And each time you'll tell me the number of my room." "Very well, Monsieur." Soon afterwards he returns, and as he passes the desk says: "Monsieur Delouit." "Number 35, Monsieur." "Thank you." A minute later, a man, extraordinarily upset, his clothes covered with mud, bleeding, his face almost not a face at all, appears at the desk: "Monsieur Delouit." "What do you mean, Monsieur Delouit? Don't try to put one over on us! Monsieur Delouit has just gone upstairs!" "I'm sorry, it's me ... I've just fallen out of the window. What's the number of my room, please?"

— ANDRÉ BRETON, *NADJA*

Nadja was taken to a madhouse in 1928. Someplace in the French countryside where ordinary people, those fortunate enough to have escaped scrutiny, who have avoided so far in their lives being similarly judged and sentenced and dismissed from the greater society, will not be reminded of their own failings by the screams of the outcast.

It is reasonable to suppose that by that time there could not be much difference for Nadja between the inside of a sanitarium and the outside—but Nadja was here, she left something of herself. Certainly she's dead by now, buried in a field behind an insane asylum, cats screwing on her grave.

The day she threatened to jump from the window of her room in the Hotel Sphinx on the Boulevard Magenta I should have known she was not a fake. Who can tell the genuine mad from the fake? Nadja could. She was always pointing them out to me. In a café she'd whisper, "Look at her. Biting her nails. Pretending to be waiting for someone. She's a fake. Her lovers disappear." "But how can you tell," I'd ask. "Look at my eyes," Nadja would say. "Can you see the way they are lit from behind? I'm dangerous. To be avoided."

Who was Nadja? What was the significance of Nadja in my life? Why does she return, a constant, though I've neither seen nor heard of or from her in fifty years?

I saw a woman in a marketplace in a Mexican city, Mérida, perhaps, in the Yucatán, twenty years ago or so. She resembled

Nadja, or what she might have looked like, according to my idea of Nadja had she still been alive, let alone an inhabitant of a jungle town in Mexico. I followed her as she moved from stand to stand, inspecting the fruits, dresses, beads, kitchen knives, crucifixes. Was this a woman or a phantom? Her gray hair was worn long and thick and fell across her face so that her features were indistinct, shadowed. Nadja had been blonde, with the short, curled haircut of the day, a brief nose, sharp black hawk's eyes, a long mouth with slender lips, purple, that grinned in one corner only. This hag in the marketplace was fat, toothless, I would say, judging by the line of her jaw, dark-skinned. Nadja had been white as the full moon of February over Venice, almost emaciated, seldom ate, with a full mouth of teeth, crooked but strong. She was capable of cracking open with ease in one swift bite a stalk of Haitian sugarcane.

How could I imagine this hideous, crumbling jungle creature to be Nadja? Some feeling made me follow until, crossing a busy street, I lost sight of her. I panicked and looked around wildly. She was gone and I was forced to suppress a great scream of pain. Unused to this severe sort of anxiety, I battled to control my emotions, there in the midst of a crowd of Indians.

It was what Nadja had meant when she stuck her tongue into my ear as we rode in a cab along the Boulevard Raspail. As quickly as she'd done it she withdrew to the opposite corner of the seat and said, staring blankly ahead, "To me nothing is more terrifying than the curse of self-fulfillment."

What did Nadja do before we met? I asked her many times and mostly she would avoid answering by laughing and kissing me, adjusting my tie, or brushing my lapels. She did tell me she was born in Belgium, near Ghent, and that her father raised flowers. She went to the local school, in a convent, and moved to Paris when she was seventeen. She met a man, unidentified, got married, gave birth to a daughter, who promptly died of pneumonia. Those were facts, according to Nadja. The man was gone soon after the daughter.

Other than that there was little Nadja would admit. None of it was important, she said. "Not to you!" She instructed me to invent her story, it was all the same, unrelated to today. "Who is the hero of a film that has at its center a peacock flying through and landing in the snow?" Nadja asks, licking my chin as if she were here.

I must recall how and why I became involved with Nadja. I was walking along the Rue Vaugirard, preparing to turn into the Luxembourg, when I saw a woman standing in front of a butcher's shop desperately examining the contents of her purse. I say desperately because there were lines of great consternation on her face, as if she had misplaced and was frantically searching for the ticket that would allow her to claim a side of beef she'd pawned or left to be laundered. The weather was foul, it was early November and it was raining. The air was ugly, full of wood smoke and water, black, brown and gray. The woman, who was

Nadja, was a disconcerting sight, her hair matted, stockings torn, coat soaked. I approached her immediately and asked if I might be of service.

"This is an evil afternoon," she said. She looked at me. "Can you buy me a drink? There are ravens everywhere now. Even in the shops, in the road. The government is full of them, as you no doubt are already aware. What would a government be without its ravens?" She stared at me with horrible yellow eyes. There was no possibility of refusal. "Of course," I said, and Nadja smiled, a sweet, genuine smile, and gently took my arm.

Nadja had a harelip. Have I mentioned that? Or had been born with a harelip. She'd had it fixed, but that was the reason for her lopsided grin that added so inexplicably to Nadja's desirability.

She disliked being thought of as foolish, though she often sought to contribute to the common good by committing foolish acts, such as disrobing in the Louvre in front of the *Mona Lisa*. For that "act of valor," as Nadja referred to it, she spent several days in jail, not having the money to pay the fine for being a public nuisance.

Following the incident at the Louvre, Nadja made a similar gesture of liberation on the Avenue d'Iena near the German Club. The Germans, she claimed, would not have her arrested; instead, Nadja said, they would pretend to ignore her. Then came the affair at Trocadero where Nadja disrobed and poured a bucket of red paint over her head. Neither time was she detained. The *Mona Lisa* episode had made her famous for the moment and her exploits of this order were no longer effective. Trocadero was Nadja's final mention in the newspapers. After that hers was a presence of secrets.

adja had a habit of laughing at the wrong moment. Someone would be in the midst of telling a story, approaching a crucial point, and Nadja would begin to laugh, softly at first, then gradually increase the level of laughter to a kind of shrill cry, shocking all those present and of course preventing the narrator from finishing his tale. This phenomenon would not occur always, but often enough so that I would be on edge whenever we were in the company of others. Several times I was forced to escort Nadja out of the room until she regained her self-control.

The unpredictable laughter was not her only social aberration. Nadja refused to be photographed. True, photographs of Nadja do exist, but they were taken surreptitiously, without her knowledge; usually when she was drunk.

Contrary to what most of my acquaintances thought at the time, Nadja was the least mysterious person I have ever met. Everything about her was obvious. Her motives were plain, she desired love, sanity, color—all healthy pursuits. Failure on any one count can hardly be held against Nadja. Disgrace, after all, is merely a manifestation of value. The price of anything is always set in advance. Nadja made me see this. Truth is perhaps more horrible than anyone would dare admit.

She was standing there in the dream, the gun still in her hand pointing down at the body when the cops broke in. It was Nadja with a Barbara Stanwyck hairdo in a black robe, a silk one with gold brocade on the wide lapels. "I shot him in the face," she said, "and he tumbled like laundry down a chute." Those were her exact words. They were fresh in my mind when I woke up. The name of the movie was *Riffraff,* that much I could remember. But it wasn't real, it was a dream, right? I hadn't seen Nadja in four years, and I knew who the man on the floor had to be.

One morning Nadja awoke and could not see out of her right eye. She sent a *pneu* asking me to meet her at the Café des Oiseaux that afternoon. "It's awful and wonderful," Nadja said as soon as I sat down at her table. "There is a cloud in my eye, floating across the center."

"Is it any particular color?" I asked.

"Red," said Nadja. "Like a veil of blood."

"Perhaps it is blood," I said. "Have you made arrangements to see a doctor?"

"Doctors can only destroy," Nadja said. "Have you a cigarette?"

I gave her one, lit it and watched her blow out the smoke.

"Usually cigarette smoke is blue," she said. "Mixed with the red it's actually quite beautiful, like two ghost ships passing through one another on the rolling sea."

I asked Nadja what she intended to do about this problem.

"Nothing," she said. "So now I have one normal eye and one very interesting eye. The left shall be the practical side, the ordinary eye, useful and necessary. The right shall be the dream side, the indefinable, the exquisite and ungraspable. The right eye is my entrance to a drifting, unstable world ruled by color and magic. Nothing is absolute there, it is a true wilderness. Covered by this thin red veil realities are made bearable by their vagueness."

I suggested to Nadja that the presence of blood in her eye, if indeed that was what it was, might be a sign of a more serious condition, a remark that caused her to explode with laughter.

Who was Madame Sacco? Unlike Madame Blavatsky no religion was founded in her name, and also unlike the Russian she was not a charlatan. Her real name was Paulette Tanguy, born in Belleville. She set up shop as Mme. Sacco on the Rue des Usines several months after the death of her third husband, an Italian, whose name I've forgotten, though I do not believe it was Sacco. In any case, he was seldom mentioned, and neither was she very forthcoming regarding his two predecessors. As to how

Mme. Sacco acquired her gift of clairvoyance, I never knew. She was never mistaken about me and I trusted her completely.

Mme. Sacco knew of Nadja's existence prior to my ever mentioning her. When Mme. Sacco told me about my preoccupation with a woman named "Hélène," I was necessarily astonished. Only a day before Nadja had said to me, seemingly apropos of nothing, "I am Hélène." These women were already connected! My reputation in certain circles for naiveté was apparently not altogether undeserved.

They did not, however, get along well. Nadja distrusted clairvoyants—"seers" she called them, rudely. "Even if they know what they're talking about," Nadja said, "even if their predictions are accurate, what right have they to inform?"

Mme. Sacco sensed immediately Nadja's hostility, and her performance in Nadja's presence was subdued. "There is a great deal I could tell you about this woman," Mme. Sacco said after Nadja had departed, "but she is opposed to it and therefore I cannot pursue her. I do know," and here Mme. Sacco smiled, "that she is dishonest, she feigns madness and is a danger to you."

"Do you mean," I asked, "that Nadja is sane? That she intends to harm me?"

"Oh no," Mme. Sacco said, smiling even more handsomely than before, "she is genuinely deranged. Her pretending is the way she fools herself. As to harm, consider what you already do to yourself. This Nadja is a brief disruption in your life."

Walking away from Mme. Sacco's I heard laughter coming from above me. I looked up and saw a boy sitting on a windowsill, playing with a live monkey. It's me, I thought. I am the monkey.

Nadja, why is it so difficult to remember exactly what you looked like? Your precise words escape me also. My re-creations are passable but not accurate. You made me examine my actions, forced me to consider possibilities other than the obvious. I am desperate now for the absolute taste of you.

I am in my studio at one minute past four o'clock in the afternoon, listening to the traffic pass in the street below my open windows. The sky is solidly grey with perhaps a stripe of white. I am embarrassed by my eagerness for night, the darkness, which I never used to be.

One evening in Père Lachaise, as we strolled among the graves, you began to sing—some children's song, I believe—and I was horrified. I dared not mention the fact to you, knowing you would ridicule my timidity; but I could not suppress the unholy feeling I derived from your merrily singing in the cemetery. Virtually everything you did disturbed, upset, surprised me. And yet I suffer.

Wherever Nadja is must be a better place than this, especially for her. I prefer to imagine Nadja in paradise, satisfied at last with the circumstances of her existence. She could never be happy in a conventional life, better that she is allowed the latitude of feeling beyond desire. That her behavior was considered bizarre, her appearance unsightly, and found herself rejected on her own terms, could not have given Nadja much hope for even an acceptable afterlife.

I recall the time Nadja decided she would be an artist, a painter. She borrowed money from me for materials and did not leave her room at the Hotel Sphinx for several days. At the end of her siege Nadja emerged with one painting, which she showed to me at the Dôme. It was a self-portrait, *Nadja Among the Carnivores,* she called it. In the painting Nadja was depicted nude, walking in a street surrounded by ghoulish figures: huge goblins with beaks, monstrous dark shapes, devils with pitchforks, deformed crones, a conglomeration of hideous, Bosch-like characters. The style was, as one might imagine, crude, the technique primitive. One could not, however, deny its power, the unsettling effect of the painting.

I told Nadja that I was impressed by the force of her work, and that I would gladly purchase the painting from her. She refused my offer. "It is not for sale," she said. "Now that you've seen it, I can destroy it." I begged her not to, but at that moment she began tearing the canvas apart, shredding it into strips. "Now," Nadja said, smiling, "I have been an artist. You are my witness. I never have to prove myself again."

My feeling about Nadja is ultimately one of sadness, loss, but not without a certain degree of satisfaction in having kept faithful to my perception of her intentions. I do not pretend to have understood Nadja, though I remain to verify her existence.

As we were walking together along the Quai d'Heure Bleue on a November afternoon, Nadja stopped and pointed to the river.

"November is the first of the Suicide Months. Look there, in the middle of the Seine, I am drowning and boats pass oblivious to my distress."

Here in the fading afternoon light, the world spinning senselessly as always, besieged by despair and unreasonable notions, I recall Nadja's succinct admonition, "Prepare."

THE TUNISIAN NOTEBOOK

– AUTHOR'S PREFACE –

I n April of 1914, the Swiss painters August Macke, Paul Klee and Louis René Moilliet embarked on a journey to North Africa to "capture the Mediterranean light." The trip lasted about two weeks, during which time they traveled from Marseilles to Tunis–St. Germain, to Sidi Bou Said, to Carthage, to Hammamet, to Kairouan, and back to Tunis. Klee kept and later published his "Diary of Trip to Tunisia," which, according to Moilliet, Klee had endeavored to keep in a formal, literary style, resulting in the description of certain incidents being exaggerated or manufactured in keeping with Klee's vision of how events should properly have proceeded.

That same year, shortly after the outbreak of World War I, Macke was killed in action. It was not until 1979, sixty-five years after the Tunisian excursion, that this imaginary notebook, containing August Macke's own diary of the trip, was discovered. It provides an interesting contrast to Klee's perceptions, as well as being a valuable and illuminating document in its own right.

"Every people has its own manner of feeling, of telling lies, of producing art ...One way of lying drives me to the next one."

— AUGUST MACKE

"One always has to spoil a picture a little bit, in order to finish it."

— EUGÈNE DELACROIX

SUNDAY, APRIL 5, NOON, MARSEILLES. Arrived in Marseilles early this morning after travelling by ship from Hilterfingen to Thun, then by train to Bern, where I changed to the Southern Express. Throughout the journey I have been thinking of Elisabeth, and wish now I had insisted she accompany me, despite Louis and Paul. Never again. At least there is the consolation of her having already seen Tunisia, but I cannot help feeling it would be better were we together.

Perhaps my mood will change once I have met up with Louis and Paul. They may be here now. I look forward to seeing Moilliet—after all, it is because of an invitation from his friend Jaeggi, the good doctor from Bern, now of Tunis, that this trip has come about. With Klee it's different; we don't always get along, not only personally but professionally. He doesn't like my poking fun at "theory." Klee is already a fine artist, but he's so premeditated about everything. In deference to Louis I'll do my best not to antagonize Klee, at least so long as he doesn't begin touting Kandinsky to me! Will try to keep painterly discussion to a minimum, stick to the example of Cézanne and Delaunay. Hot, tired, hungry—the usual condition. Downstairs for refreshment.

APRIL 5, 11 P.M. Marseilles is a miracle of color! After eating I walked around the town, admiring the flowers, boats in the harbor, the clean, distinct whites, blues, yellows, greens, and reds. A healthy breeze came up, which diminished my fatigue. Noticed a tall, striking woman with an unusual hairdo—amber curls piled high and spilling over her forehead—and followed her. She met some people outside of an arena where a bullfight was about to begin. As I'd never witnessed a bullfight, I followed them in. The admission was cheap, a couple of francs.

The arrangement of shapes and contrasts in the crowd was spectacular, and far more interesting to watch than the spectacle itself. The bull was not killed but so poked and battered about that by the time the devils had done with the game it might have been kinder to murder the beast and spare it the misery of recovery, if indeed recovery is possible.

The bull began a thick, brown hue, with almost yellow horns, and became progressively darker during the ordeal. By the finish his hide was greyish black, the horns sandy white. I forced myself to watch it all. I completely forgot the tall woman with the red-yellow curls. It became difficult to control myself, but somehow I managed to keep from being sick.

Afterwards walked along the quais and stopped at a sidewalk table on the Vieux Port. Sat over a vermouth until I felt sufficiently recovered, then ordered a big meal, which I was just finishing when Moilliet and Klee peeked over the hedge that surrounded the restaurant and spotted me.

I was glad to see them, and felt increasingly better as I described for them the bullfight and the woman with the odd hairdo. Louis remarked that Jaeggi had quite an eye for the ladies. Klee added that he thought it only appropriate that it should have been a woman to have led me to a scene of slaughter. Louis laughed and I reminded them that the bull, in France, anyway, was allowed to survive. "You look healthy enough!" Klee said, and suggested that we go to the music hall, which we did.

Paul seemed especially to enjoy a comedy routine wherein a young man impersonated a Tyrolian girl, but neither Louis nor I were much taken by it. The performers seemed less than enthusiastic, their movements wooden and artificial, and so, too, the impression that remains, the colors somber and dim.

Walking back to the hotel I mentioned this to the others, pointing to a pair of violet birds perched on the lip of a bluish grey rainspout. "Immortal moments meant to be captured."

But I was speaking more for the benefit of Klee than Moilliet. Louis understands. It was he who paid me the greatest compliment, last December, when we first met to discuss this venture. "Until I met you," Moilliet said, "I painted the way a man looks out the window."

MONDAY, APRIL 6, 10 P.M., ABOARD THE CARTHAGE, THE MEDITERRANEAN SEA. We spent the morning exploring Marseilles. Klee was moved enough by the sights to consider staying on but Louis—"The Count," Klee calls him—regaled us with promises of greater treasures in the days ahead. Klee said the colors around Marseilles were "new." I disagreed politely: "They're only new to you because you've never seen them before." Louis got the joke but not Paul. Sometimes I think he is too serious to ever become a really great painter.

Boarded the *Carthage* at midday. A clean, freshly painted *barque*. A nice sail out of the harbor, but once in the Gulf of Lions each of us was forced, one by one, to take seasick pills. Klee's didn't work—he got them from Gabriele Münter—so I gave him some of mine, and soon he was holding up all right.

Klee knows I don't think much of him sometimes—though I don't dislike him. He's jealous of my "success." What success? I asked Louis. Because Kohler likes my paintings and gives me something for them? Paul is dedicated, he'll have his day, perhaps more than one, and it will be bigger than either Moilliet's or mine, I fear, knowing the public taste. He is by far the toughest of us three.

My unreasonable prejudice against Klee begins with his pipe. He is a pipe smoker, and I have never in my twenty-six years yet met a pipe smoker I didn't find to be a bore. Often a mean bore, the worst kind, the ones who insist on boring the hell out of you even after they've realized you're not in the least interested in what they're saying. Not that Klee is one of those—not yet anyway.

At dinner Louis and Paul ate like pigs, but I outdid them.

The seas are a steady six feet; the boat rolls, but not uncomfortably. Standing on deck tonight I could feel the sun waiting to come out.

TUESDAY, APRIL 7, 10:30 P.M. TUNIS. Klee is an early riser. By the time I came out on deck this morning he had breakfasted and begun sketching. "That's Sardinia," he told me, pointing toward the coastline.

I found Moilliet in the dining room. While we ate he told me how even as a child—they'd been schoolmates—Klee had been extraordinarily self-centered. Louis says Paul went forward and sat around with the third-class passengers for awhile. He likes to pretend he is one of them so that they will not react to him differently than they do to each other. This way, says Klee, he'll be able to capture their true expressions in his memory. He collects children's drawings, and saved many of those from his own childhood. Louis says Paul believes they hold the key to the future.

I don't mean to be going on all the time complaining about Klee and his attitudes. Perhaps there is something about him that I envy—his physical energy, or his confidence. Elisabeth is always joking about what she considers my laziness, but she only half-jokes—she must be serious or she wouldn't mention it so often. She remarks about it to guests. "Whatever will become of him when he grows old?" What she means by that I'm not certain. Perhaps I won't grow old.

It will be interesting to see what Klee accomplishes here. Actually I don't think he is half as adventuresome as I am, or even Moilliet. But he has an astonishing ability to relate objects and images historically. This evening at dinner he quoted Delacroix on North Africa—"every man I see is a Cato or Brutus"—the Greco-Roman world incarnate. Paul is more well read than I. But reading is more tiring than anything!

We spotted the African coast late in the day, at what seemed the pinnacle of the afternoon heat. It was white-green. Not until Sidi Bou Said did we discern a land-shape, a hill covered with white dots—houses in regular up-and-down rows.

The boat navigated a narrow inlet which led to a long canal. It was white-hot and dead feeling, the water unmoving, though we could clearly see the Arabs along the shore in turbans and robes. We stood at the rail to try and catch a bit of wind, but the boat moved terribly slowly and the air was terrifically hot and sticky.

Klee commented ecstatically about the picturesqueness of the shoreline, and talked excitedly about the prospect of painting the Arab faces. I am not quite sure how to regard these remarks of his. It's as if he's just another philistine standing before an exquisite view, saying, "Beautiful, beautiful, beautiful," which reaction is the cheapest kind of traditional expression. But I know he's not. The manner of reacting varies not only with race but with personality. The Egyptians, the Chinese, the men of the Gothic age, Memling, Snyders, Cézanne, Mozart. The type of reaction varies as the human condition varies. Today it is impossible for an artist to work as a Renaissance or a Pompeiian artist worked. Most important is the conclusion: A Cézanne still life is as real as the wall on which it stands.

Dr. Jaeggi and his family—wife, daughter—met our boat and took us into Tunis, all of us squashed into their little yellow automobile. Jaeggi is a wonderful fellow, my age, very agreeable, just as Moilliet said he was. Louis likened him to Dr. Gachet, van Gogh's doctor friend at Auvers. The Arabs call him "Father Jaeggi," and act like fawning children around him. He is an obstetrician. In Bern he was, at an extremely early age, a prominent surgeon. I meant to ask Louis—or Jaeggi himself—why he came to Tunisia. I must remember to do so tomorrow. His wife and daughter are lovely—the girl has a dancing face.

Jaeggi took us to his house in St. Germain—he keeps an office in Tunis, at No. 2 Bab-el-Allouch, his card says—where we rested and recovered from the intense heat under large fans, and then had a superb meal prepared by Frau Jaeggi and the servant Ahmed, a lithe, chocolate fellow with a brilliant smile. Jaeggi says that he, Ahmed, is a genuine artist, a good one.

After dinner Jaeggi drove me into the city to the Hôtel de France—the others are staying at the house—and saw that I was properly settled before leaving me. On the way in the car he told me how pleased he was that we—through Moilliet—had accepted his invitation, and that I, too, was welcome to stay in St. Germain. I thanked him and explained that, unlike Louis and Paul, I had a patron, and could afford the luxury of a hotel, adding that it would be less work for Ahmed and Frau Jaeggi. He said I was welcome to change my mind at any time.

The night air is sweet and warm. Tunisia is already a pleasant surprise.

WEDNESDAY APRIL 8, MIDNIGHT, ST. GERMAIN. Louis and Paul arrived early this morning with Jaeggi, in his car. I hadn't had breakfast as yet so they accompanied me to a café near the marketplace. While I ate they shopped at nearby stalls—the souks.

Jaeggi sat and had a coffee, telling me he's never bothered to get a license, here or in Bern. A driver's license, that is. He says he's never been reprimanded for not having one, not even when stopped by the police for some reason. They see his identification as a doctor and make their apologies for having delayed him. Why bother with a driver's permit when a medical certificate will do? Jaeggi's an extraordinary man.

Tunisia is a real world, he told me, not an artificial one like Europe, with its parks and gardens, "Paint what you see," he said, "it's enough." If by "real" he means no derby hats or Paris styles, he is correct.

Moilliet came over to tell us of a funeral procession. We could hear the wailing and moaning, and then a cart drawn by six scrawny mules clattered slowly past the café, a blue and gold coffin strapped onto it. Louis followed after it, fascinated. Ever since old Gobat's death he has been exceedingly passionate about funerals.

The rest of us went along and watched as the burial was accomplished in a little field just beyond the market. Klee kept his smile fixed just so. He thinks Louis is a bit of a fool and that I am too set in my ways. He's right, but so what?

After a short tour courtesy of Dr. Jaeggi, he went to his office and I decided to explore the native quarter on my own, enlisting the aid of a policeman who observed me buying charcoals and paints. I asked him if he could guide me to the more interesting spots, the whorehouses, drug dens, etc. Who should know better than a police officer where to go?

For not very much money he agreed to show me around and, presumably, abandoned his official duties for the remainder of the afternoon. Klee refused to go along, though I hadn't asked him to come with me. He seemed upset and wanted to make his disapproval known, but I didn't pay him much attention. He and Moilliet went off to explore some mosques.

Abdoul, the policeman, earned his francs, showing me, in fact, more than I could absorb in an afternoon. I made dozens of sketches, several of the prostitutes in a house on Rue Rouge, lounging on divans in negligees, their necks strung with pearls, smoking and joking with one another. They were very familiar with Abdoul, as I'd guessed they'd be. I gave them each a sketch of themselves and they seemed quite taken by them. I promised to return soon, without my drawing materials, and they all laughed. To my surprise they appeared to be very bright girls.

There is so much here to attract the eye! Ornate, arched gates, bazaars, the market, terraces with awnings, tents, domes of mosques, mules, camels, and these beautiful, brown-skinned people.

In the evening drove with Jaeggi out to St. Germain for dinner. He would like Klee and I to paint the interior of his studio. We agreed to do so. I am staying the night, much to the apparent displeasure of the housemaid, a heavy, sweaty girl from Aargau, who did a poor job of preparing my bed. I mentioned this to Louis a few moments ago in the hall. "There's one thing the Aargau girl does know how to do," he said, "to draw a bath! That she does perfectly."

THURSDAY APRIL 9, 11 P.M., TUNIS. After breakfast Jaeggi drove Klee and me into town, left us at the hotel, and continued on to his surgery. Paul insisted that I accompany him to the harbor to paint. I made a number of small paintings, but was so bothered by the coal dust in my eyes and in the watercolors that I was forced to stop. Klee worked on despite the conditions, and in the face of taunts by crew members of a French torpedo boat tied up nearby, who cursed us in broken German.

I ate lunch alone in the same café as yesterday and then wandered on my own until I found the tomb of a Marabu, a Moslem saint. My policeman told me yesterday they were everywhere because Arab saints were always buried on the spot where they died. There are many in Tunis and, apparently, in and around Sidi Bou Said. I did a painting of the entranceway, without interference from dust, sailors, or fellow artists!

Met Louis and Paul for supper and afterwards went with them to a concert Arabe. They are real tourists, as obvious as though they wore large red badges emblazoned with the word itself. Moilliet, because of his naiveté, is the easier to accept, but Klee looks down on the natives. His condescending conversation is insufferable. There is nothing barbaric about belly dancing. The women and their glistening skin adorned with multifarious decorations form a symmetry that is a kinetic delight. Tunisia is not a prudish country. Paul pretends he is undisturbed by this kind of performance; Louis exults. I am someplace in between.

FRIDAY APRIL 10, 9 P.M., TUNIS. Made sixty sketches today! A truly inspired one for me. I share Klee's respect for the images of childhood and children's works of art. To produce true art one must experience a rebirth, as does nature with each fresh season. One must tap the flow of nature in order to be able to create art in a musical, Mozartian manner.

The day was filled with such a lively, pristine, childlike light that I had no thoughts of eating. Upon arising I dressed quickly, gathered up my paints and pencils and the paper I brought from Switzerland, and hurried out into the street without bothering about washing. By noon I'd done two dozen drawings and felt fresh as ever.

I stopped in the market to buy some fruit but instead fell into conversation with an Italian photographer who showed me a portfolio of amazing pictures. I bought fifteen of them, portraits of women in many imaginative positions, which I showed around the dinner table this evening at the house of Captain Lecoq. Lecoq, a friend of Jaeggi's, is a French officer who is quite popular with the Arabs since he has taken their side against the government in Paris. He says after ten years in Tunis he feels more like an Arab than a Frenchman—Lecoq is not an ordinary official, he is quite outgoing. He practically licked the photographs and made some appropriately wicked remarks concerning the poses. After dinner he asked me if I'd yet visited any of the houses in the Quarter. When I told him I had, but only to make drawings, he looked at me strangely. Then I told him I was in the company of a policeman. Lecoq laughed and said the policeman must have been very amused. "The behavior of foreigners never ceases to amaze."

SATURDAY, APRIL 11, 11:45 P.M., ST. GERMAIN. Spent a couple of hours in and around the market this morning looking for something to bring Elisabeth. I bought her several uniquely detailed pieces of embroidery and an amber necklace—a Mohammedan rosary—with a stone seal from Achat inlaid with mysterious signs, and I bought a pair of yellow slippers for myself. Wrote her a letter, the first since our arrival, and a short one at that. There are too many things to do and see to spend one's time writing letters.

Jaeggi called for me at the hotel about three, and we drove out to St. Germain. Sat on the terrace drinking wine and talking with Jaeggi—a pleasant afternoon. He is actually a bit younger than I, a renowned surgeon, and yet he insists on calling me the "accomplished" one.

Jaeggi told me the story of Lecoq's infatuation with a thirteen-year-old Arab girl. Apparently she came to him every day for six months until her father found out about it. Because Lecoq gave the girl money now and then the mother begged her husband not to do anything—and of course as an officer of the French garrison Lecoq commands substantial political power. But the father went berserk and attacked Lecoq with a knife. Lecoq shot him dead. Immediately thereafter he was given a holiday leave, which he spent in France. He returned to Tunis a month later, by which time both the girl and her mother had disappeared.

Klee came in from working on the beach. Louis was sketching the sunset from the balcony. Jaeggi suggested we decorate Easter eggs for the holiday tomorrow, which we did. Ahmed brought them in and helped make the designs. His eggs were far more intricately fashioned than any of ours, supporting Jaeggi's judgment of his talent.

After another generous and well-prepared dinner, Klee and I set to the dining room wall. Klee contented himself with a few doodles in the corners, while I marked out a six-foot square in the middle in which I depicted a market scene—a small black donkey laden with baskets of oranges, flanked by two red-tarbooshed Arab drivers. Jaeggi seemed more than a little pleased with our work.

Moilliet opened a bottle of brandy for the occasion, and insisted we finish it before retiring. Curiously, I don't feel at all drunk, only fatigued from the constant heat, which I doubt I could ever get used to.

EASTER SUNDAY, APRIL 12, 4 P.M., TUNIS. A poor day for me. Holidays are not the time to be away from home. I fear I miss Elisabeth and my sons too much. Tried to rouse myself from the doldrums at Jaeggi's, drew a picture of his daughter and gave it to her—her parents will frame it and hang it in her room—but was unsuccessful. I dare not write home while I am in this condition.

I joined feebly in the hunt for the eggs. Klee was upset that the colors came off on our fingers, but nobody else seemed to mind.

Jaeggi drove me into Tunis and deposited me at the hotel so that I could rest without being disturbed before our journey tomorrow to Hammamet. There is a measurable amount of moisture in the air.

TUESDAY APRIL 14, 10:30 P.M., HAMMAMET. Slept all day yesterday, therefore no entry in the notebook. Had to postpone our travel plans until today. It must have been a slight case of influenza that brought on my melancholia.

Louis and Paul were in good spirits throughout the trip. They seemed to have been inspired by the dawn departure. The ancient locomotive wound slowly through stretches of desert broken occasionally by pathetic patches of forest. Moilliet (with his bottle of brandy—he is not without one these days) and Klee were enraptured by the—to me—sparse scenery.

Outside Hammamet station we spent half an hour watching a camel, instructed by a veiled young woman, draw water from a well by walking back and forth pulling a rope attached to a bucket. A time-tested method. Klee would have remained there forever had Louis and I not threatened to go on without him. Paul worships the primitive.

Spent the day with watercolors in the main cemetery. Unlike in Tunis, here we are free to explore them. Fabulous cactuses tower over us. From a distance they resemble the great dusty buildings of an abandoned city. I set up my things on a small hill from which I could observe the crooked coastline and benefit from a gentle but steady breeze.

Found lodging in a rooming house run by a tough old dame who claims she's French, from Nice, but she's an Arab. Smokes black tobacco. Her fingers are deeply stained. For dinner she offered us cow liver, so we went to a café instead. The food there was not very appealing either, but we had a light meal while being "entertained" by a blind nasal singer accompanied by a young boy on a drum.

After dinner we followed the noise of a band to a little street fair, where we watched one fakir let a cobra bite him on the nose and another devour live scorpions.

Louis and I finished off his brandy, the melancholic's companion.

WEDNESDAY, APRIL 15, JUST PAST MIDNIGHT, KAIROUAN. Quite a trip today. This morning trekked to Bir-bou-rekba from Hammamet, earning curious stares from berobed Arabs along the road. Passersby spat greetings to us, nodding and smiling. Three European gentlemen on foot, wearing suits and straw hats, packing gear on their backs—surely as ridiculous a sight as they've ever seen. It was Louis who insisted we walk, to "gain the feel" of the province.

It was actually quite a short distance, perhaps two kilometers, to the Bir-bou-rekba station, where we boarded a train to Kalaa-srira. There we stopped for lunch at a dusty café run by a black Arab madman in a torn red djilaba. Dozens of wild chickens ran amongst the tables searching for drops of food in the dust. Moilliet was undisturbed by the situation—he smiled and sipped his brandy. Klee and I attempted to order, but the proprietor chased insanely around after the chickens, shouting threats on the life of his neighbor, to whom the fowl belonged.

Soon all the customers were laughing and taunting the restaurant owner. I took the remnants of a meal from an abandoned nearby table and scattered the bits on the ground, causing a crazed clucking, screeching, dust-swirling stampede. The chickens were now hopping onto the tables and chairs and the poor proprietor was beside himself.

He yelled at me to stop encouraging the beasts, to please not throw them bread crumbs. I responded indignantly: "But sir, I wouldn't dare to feed them bread crumbs, I'm giving them cheese!"

After that the unfortunate man gave up. All we managed to pry from his kitchen was some weak coffee, for which we reluctantly paid three francs. At that moment our train entered the station and we embarked for Kairouan. After a brief stopover in Acouda, which from the train appeared as a raging storm of flies and dust, we arrived in Kairouan in mid-afternoon.

Found a French hotel in the center of town—the Marseilles—ate, drank, slept until evening. No work. Tonight attended a marriage feast—the daughter of the hotel proprietor and a local, apparently well-to-do businessman. A magnificent outdoor banquet: roasted lamb, chicken, dozens of unfamiliar delicacies. We ate and drank everything that was offered. Klee was ecstatic—for the first time on the trip he looked completely relaxed.

THURSDAY, APRIL 16, 8 P.M., TUNIS. The Tunisian sky in the moment before dawn is mysteriously affecting. Watching it brighten, my feeling of personal insignificance increased.

Reds, blues, yellows folded over and under one another, orange clouds merged and parted in a living collage. Finally, light, pure light, orchestrated by camel groans and dispersing shadows, a gray-pink cat without a tail stretching and rolling over in the dust.

Made a series of paintings in the morning, a herdsman in red fez and brown robe, two heavily draped women on the road to the city, date trees, domed roofs, a leopard-faced boy in the town square. This afternoon we hired a guide, who showed us through the local mosques. He expressed interest in learning German, so I taught him the words for white, black, shit, piss, fuck, eat, and how much. A sufficient vocabulary in any language.

Arrived back in Tunis at dusk. Louis joined the Jaeggis at Lecoq's, Klee went off to spend some time alone, and I took a long bath at the hotel, after which I found Paul at the Chianti restaurant and stuffed myself with pasta al pesto. Paul is planning to leave for home on Sunday. He thinks Louis intends to stay on for a few days past that. I would like to stay longer also, and will speak to Moilliet about it tomorrow.

FRIDAY, APRIL 17, 11 P.M., TUNIS. Sketched until noon in the marketplace. Thus far I've made more than thirty watercolors and dozens of drawings. Wrote a short letter—only the second since I've been gone—to Elisabeth, telling her I will be bringing some colossal things back with me. I must travel more often to exotic places! I seem able to see everything so clearly, to understand the people by an expression, a tilt of the head. Because of my unfamiliarity with them, things become more distinct.

We took an afternoon trip back to Kalaa-srira to see a mosque Klee heard about last night. Had tea and bread at the madman's café—no chickens! He must have poisoned them all. The mosque was less than spectacular, a rather ordinary facade and white-washed interior, and we were there at the wrong hour—and apparently the wrong season—to witness the angles of light that distinguished it. Moilliet and I were bored, the waste of an afternoon.

On the way to Tunis we wrestled in the train compartment —Louis and I, that is. Klee is outraged by this kind of behavior. He says the Arabs will think less of us if we act improperly; i.e., "un-European." Any manner of physical spontaneity disgusts him. I can't take too much of Klee—and he considers me facile, I know. It's just as well we don't have much time left together.

Had dinner alone in a café near the hotel, and read the first European newspaper I've seen since coming to Tunisia. My interest in that world has drastically diminished. If it weren't for the unsanitary conditions I think I should like to stay on in North Africa indefinitely.

SATURDAY, APRIL 18, AFTER MIDNIGHT, TUNIS. Just returned from a marvelous evening at Jaeggi's, where we all got drunk and made passes at everyone's wives. Louis passed around my famous Italian photographs, which were universally admired—especially by the ladies—and that got everything started. Jaeggi's other dinner guests—there were sixteen in all—had been invited, in view of our impending departure, for a farewell celebration.

I'm afraid I'm too drunk to write very much or very well. When one officer's wife asked me where I'd bought the pictures—which she called "French cards"—I told her to please take for herself her favorite one. I thought my offer would be humorously rejected, but the lady surprised me by choosing one of my own favorites and depositing it in her purse!

The rest of the day was rather dull; I remember very little other than that it rained steadily for the first time, putting the natives in a good mood.

SUNDAY, APRIL 19, 6 P.M., TUNIS. Back from seeing Klee off, third class on a rusty tub. He pretends to be happy when he's miserable, a compulsion with which I have no sympathy. The day has been taken up with farewell conversations and the gathering together of belongings. Moilliet and I will leave tomorrow for Thun via Palermo and Rome. The Jaeggis are wonderful people. They have been glad to see us, and now they're glad to see us go, which is how it should be.

Time to eat, and afterwards, perhaps a stroll in the little rain.

THE BRIEF CONFESSION OF AN UNREPENTANT EROTIC

My real name is Julius Mordecai Pincus. I am a Jew, born in the small Balkan village of Vidin, in Bulgaria, on March 31, 1885. I was the seventh of eight children, and I grew up mostly in Bucharest and Vienna. I attended school from the age of ten until I was sixteen. At seventeen I began life on my own, living first in Budapest, then Vienna, Munich, and Berlin. It was during this initial stage of independent discovery, roughly from 1902 to 1905, that I re-created myself.

At sixteen I was initiated into the rites of male/female sexual relations by a woman of fifty. Prominent in Viennese society, Anna was a wealthy, not altogether unattractive widow. She paid me to visit her; she had employed a number of other boys before it came my turn. Though Anna was well-schooled in a variety of forms of lovemaking, she preferred the oral type. She told me she was and had been since the age of eleven a chronic self-masturbator, an activity she enjoyed performing for her lovers.

I suppose my fascination with women's bodies began with Anna. She had a full, well-preserved figure, rather thick-legged. Above the nipple of her left breast was a large, dark blue, star-shaped mole. Anna referred to it as her "Egyptian wound," or "the Pharaoh's kiss."

From Anna I went on to discover the delights of Celeste, Del'Al, Mary, Hermine, Lucy, Marcelle, Claudine, Mireille, Cesarine, Andrée, Mado, Henriette, Clara, Lydis, Simone, Geneviève, Hilda, Marianne, Jeanette, Suzette, Aischa, Eliane, Paquita, Dinitia, Odile, Odette, Cleo, and others whose names do not come immediately to mind. They were and are all wonderful simply because they are women. Women are the greatest of all wonders, the most fascinating of God's secrets. Of course, I believe in God. I have always believed in God. It is God who enables me to breathe into life and death these paintings and drawings, who works my wrist and fingers, stimulates my brain, unpeels my eyes.

It is almost morning. I am sitting at the writing table in my bedroom at the Villa des Camellias. I know now that I am unable to go on. As I remarked yesterday afternoon to Dubreuil, I have worked so hard, only to be considered a freak, at best a beast, at worst a fraud. Shall I be obliged to suffer further deprecations by the pens and lips of failed artists and frightened, self-loathing weasels? I think not.

This is my brief confession. My public and private life will be remembered and memorialized by Hermine and Lucy, the only two women I have ever truly loved. My physical life is finally in my own hands. I own the future, which is as unenviable a responsibility as anyone could imagine. But this is the "time of tongue between the teeth," as the Cuban Indians say.

I have never been a man until now. Women with fingers between their legs, spectacular tropical sunsets, a red ribbon lying in the street. Who else but I can decide what is meaningful?

C ritics accuse me of drawing dirty pictures, depicting women disrespectfully, in uncouth fashion. They're fools. I have absolute reverence for these women. I am fascinated by them, astounded by their honesty and ability to survive despite a variety of cruelties having been imposed upon them. I am not so brave. And so I regard these women with admiration, inspect their habitats, closely observe and record their habits, postures, uninhibited instants, as would any proper anthropologist.

The sisters Odile and Odette, my closest companions of late, are perhaps the most perfect examples of this particular study. When they were six and four, respectively, they were raped by their father, who continued to practice upon them diverse sexual abuse until Odile, at the age of eleven, stabbed him to death while he slept. The girls were institutionalized for five years, raised by nuns and then released into the world, virtually penniless, to make their way. I discovered them a couple of years later. Odile was a prostitute and Odette worked as a washerwoman, mopping up barrooms. I took them in and employed them as models. Their figures are superb and each is unrestrained in her lovemaking. In this regard they are more than I can handle. They need constant attention and to engage in sexual activities several times a day. I offer them to my friends regularly and so manage to please everyone.

Odile and Odette remind me of the *chocolatas* of Cuba, *las negritas,* with their full lips and taunting gazes. I was happy in Cuba; the tropical light is like no other, the foliage as dense and dazzlingly beautiful as any I've seen. A kind of reptilian mystery pervades the atmosphere, a suggestion of danger slithers through the mind and is reflected in the movements of the people. These sisters of mine, were they dark instead of blonde, if they spoke rapid Spanish rather than languid French, could be Lupe and Luisa in place of Odile and Odette.

In Munich, when I was eighteen, I met a wonderful girl named Liebe—Love—whose father raised flowers. Liebe and I would wander among the flowers, touching hands, stopping here and there to kiss, and finally, finding an appropriate place and being unable to restrain ourselves any longer, we would collapse among the reds, yellows, blues, greens, violets.

During this time I worked for *Simplicissimus,* a satirical review, and decided to anagrammatize my name from Pincus to Pascin. It was then that I came upon the works of Klimt and Schiele, and realized how one might approach erotica tenderly and with humor. This was the path I chose to follow, portraying the sudden danger of lust and risking the harsh criticism that often ensues when one attempts to entertain.

My arrival in Paris on Christmas Eve of 1905 coincided, more or less, with others I felt were of a similar disposition. Among these were Libermann, Modigliani, Picasso, Kisling, and my fellow landsmen Soutine and Chagall. Each of them expressed in those days a desire to create holiness out of vulgarity. I have sought to do the same—in Munich, Berlin, Paris, New Orleans, Florida, Texas, Havana, New York, Tunis; in dance bars, offices, brothels, studios, cafés; with ink, charcoal, paint, pencil. My objective has been to delineate the perfect within the imperfect. I would not compromise in subject or form. A man's temperament is more important than his work.

I want to say that I am not evil, that I have never had an evil thought, but I don't know if this can ever be true of any person other than those born demented. I have manipulated, coerced, flattered falsely, given incorrect information, misrepresented myself, and none of this in the name of Art. What living being can deny in his soul that he has done the same?

I have been unable to marry the woman I love because she will not divorce her husband and I will not divorce my wife. Life drags on and one attempts to ignore the inevitable, to disguise ugliness, pretend not to be affected by ridicule and calumny, not recognize the symptoms of serious illness. All at once, it seems, one must succumb. My insistent attempts at immortality have resulted in a body of work anyone can contemplate without inter-ference from interpretation.

This is a cold night and I am alone. Odile and Odette await me at the café. Faint flakes of snow swirl outside the window in which Paquita's painted face and breasts are reflected. Life itself is inad-equate for my requirements. I am a demanding, selfish, foolish creature, no better than a hungry dog. Mine is a deserving fate. Poverty is hideous, madness is concrete. I am done with this at last! I am done.

No man, and above all no artist, should live for more than forty-five years. If by then he has not already given his best, he will achieve nothing more after that age. There is no cure for this relentless, self-inflicted terror. It is ultimately an artificial life. Reality is what remains.

THE YELLOW PALACE

My name is Antonio Pulli. I am seventy-six years old in this year of 1406 by the Arabic calendar. For the past three and a half decades I have operated a restaurant in Cairo. For a quarter of a century prior to that my main occupation was as companion and aide to Farouk, the former king of Egypt. I was known popularly as Farouk's procurer, mainly of women. While it is true that in his mature years Farouk maintained a sizeable appetite for women, many of whom I assisted him in locating, our association began when I was sixteen and he was eight years old. My father, Francesco Pulli, was the court electrician at Ras-el-Tin Palace in Alexandria during the reign of Farouk's father, Sultan Fuad. I repaired a toy train of Farouk's and from that day forward we were inseparable.

I was eventually knighted by Farouk—a *bey* in Arabic—and there was nothing of his activities to which I was not privy until the moment of his exile, at which time I was imprisoned by the rebels. They broke into my quarters at Abdin Palace and discovered the glass case containing thirty hooks, on each of which hung a key appended with a tag detailing the name of a particular woman, her address, and a description of the entrance to her house. Among these keys were several to rooms at Cairo hotels, such as the Semiramis and the Heliopolis House. That Farouk enjoyed the company of women is undeniable. I would estimate that during his lifetime he consorted in one fashion or another with more than five thousand women, more than even his revered grandfather, Farouk's idol, Ismail the Magnificent. Farouk was unrivaled in the pursuit of his libidinous pastime. An example: When he built al-Moussa Hospital in Alexandria he had constructed on the top floor seventeen lavishly furnished rooms, each with a grand view of the Mediterranean, solely in order to have a private place to bring his women. Never have I seen a place where the contrast of suffering and pleasure was so immediately evident.

It would be too easy, however, to dismiss Farouk as a selfish, shallow man or an unfeeling ruler. He was probably not mistaken when he said to me and Mohammed Hassan, his Nubian chauffeur, shortly before his final departure for Capri, "In this country of twenty million souls, I do not have a single friend." But there are reasons for this, and the fault lies not solely with Farouk himself. Mohammed Hassan, who has for many years now operated a hotel at Khartoum in the Sudan, could testify to this as well. Farouk's life might have been entirely different had he not had to assume the crown at the age of sixteen.

When Farouk was a boy he displayed sincere interest in academic areas: the sciences, literature, music. At fifteen he was sent to England to complete his education. Farouk studied at the Royal Military Academy at Woolwich, where he was attended by four men from the Sultan's court: Ahmed Mohammed Hassanein Bey, the Minister Plenipotentiary; General Aziz el-Misri Pasha, a military adviser; Saleih Hashim, professor of Arabic and Islamic science; and Dr. Kafrawi, his personal physician. All of these men reported that Farouk was acquitting himself admirably at school. Farouk was a good horseman, and he spoke fluent French and English, in addition to Arabic. He represented Egypt at the funeral of King George V while he was in England, and the reports were that his behavior in that circumstance was exemplary. I have no doubt that had Farouk been able to develop gradually his own personality he would have become a respected and generous king.

Sultan Fuad died barely a year after Farouk left for England. He was brought back immediately after his father's death and was forced to assume the kingdom of Mohammed Ali, the Great, the Father of modern Egypt, hereditary vizier of Egypt and Governor of Nubia, Sennar, Kordofan, and Darfur. Mohammed Ali's grandson, Ismail, expanded the kingdom; it was Ismail who built an opera house and commissioned Giuseppe Verdi to write *Aida*. Fuad was Ismail's son, and he did not prepare Farouk adequately for the role of king. The Egypt over which Farouk assumed leadership was one rampant with disease: tuberculosis, malaria, and syphilis were common. Babies' eyes were covered with sores and flies. Unfaithful wives were cut up and thrown into the Nile; peasant women would eat the polluted Nile mud as part of their religious belief that it would assure easy childbirth, and they would smear the mud on their bodies as a sign of sorrow following the death of a loved one. These practices spread bacterial disease such as bilharzia and hookworm. Primitive as Egypt appears now, it was then even more so.

Farouk, of course had grown up in luxurious circumstances, mainly at Ras-el-Tin Palace. His mother, Queen Nazli, was a Franco-Egyptian, the eldest daughter of Abdul Rahim Sabri, and she had been raised in Paris. Farouk's nursemaid, a Turkish woman named Ah'sha Galshan, had been carefully chosen for her bountiful breasts. She used often to complain about Farouk's powerful jaw that left her nipples sore! Biting women's nipples remained one of Farouk's greatest pleasures. It was Ah'sha Galshan and the assistant court chamberlain, Ahmed Hassanein Pasha, who raised the young Farouk. The Sultan was thirty years older than Queen Nazli, and neither of them paid much attention to the future king.

Fuad lay in state in Cairo at the Mosque el-Rifai, where Farouk accepted the condolences and best wishes of world leaders. He took up residence in Abdin Palace at sixteen. Mohammed Altabii, an Egyptian journalist, wrote of Farouk at that time: "He acquires admiration and respect for his person, without resource to his crown. He is intellectually mature, has vast culture, and is well-spoken in public. The love of the people for Farouk rises daily, and this from a people that has always been disappointed in its leaders. Only Farouk has not disappointed them." And the Prime Minister of Lebanon declared Farouk "not only the king of Egypt, but the King of all the Arabs."

Egypt in the 1930s, of course, was occupied by the British, and Farouk had to learn how to deal with this presence in the face of fierce Moslem objection. Nazli had no love for the Arab masses; being half French, she considered herself a European and spent much of her time in Paris and Switzerland. Farouk's four sisters—Fawzia, who would later become the first wife of the Shah of Iran, Faiza, Faika and Fathia—knew nothing of the world. Farouk had to depend entirely on his father's advisers, who, naturally, counseled the young monarch to leave the administration of the government to them.

So Farouk found himself with a kingdom to amuse himself in. He enlisted me as his "right-hand man," as the Americans say. Along with Mohammed Hassan as chauffeur, Pietro della Valle, the palace assistant barber, and two Albanian bodyguards, I was closest to Farouk. We comprised the king's coterie, his most trusted servants. When he was seventeen, Farouk married Safinaz, who was only fifteen, and whose name he changed to Farida, in keeping with his father Fuad's policy of beginning names of royalty with the letter F. Farida was coerced into the marriage by her parents. She did not want to marry Farouk, and told me before the wedding, "I have read the story of Joan of Arc and

I feel the same as she when she knew that she would be burned at the stake the next day."

The marriage was a disaster. Both Farouk and Farida were far too young to understand what a marriage was supposed to be, so they ended up living very separate lives. That Farida bore Farouk only daughters and not a son did not help matters. And when Farouk's mother, Nazli, entered into an at-first secret marriage with Ahmed Hassanein, Farouk's view of the trustworthiness of women plummeted to an unrecoverable depth.

Farouk's biggest problem, in his own mind at least, was the diminutive size of his penis. Though Farouk was six feet tall and of muscular proportions as a young man, his penis, when fully erect, measured no more than two inches in length. This fact, perhaps more than any other, contributed to his obsession with sex. As he grew fatter over the years, exceeding three hundred pounds by the age of thirty, it became virtually impossible for Farouk to successfully have sexual intercourse with a woman. Annie Berrier, a French showgirl who resided for a time in Cairo, explained to Farouk that there were methods other than intercourse by which a woman might be satisfied. It was due to Annie Berrier that Farouk acquired the nickname "Talented Tongue." This appellation pleased Farouk enormously; he made no secret of his indebtedness to Annie for educating him in the more sophisticated forms of lovemaking. Farouk told me that with Annie it was even possible for him to enjoy so-called normal sexual congress. Apparently she was extraordinarily adept at the act, managing to accomplish with Farouk what few others could. The King spoke highly of her always and was deeply saddened when she returned to France.

During World War II, Farouk became convinced that the British would lose. Though he had been educated in England and affected various British mannerisms, especially in speech, Farouk felt that Rommel's Afrika Korps and Graziani's Italian armies could not be defeated. Farouk often inveighed against the swaggering racist Australian and New Zealand troops that were stationed in Egypt. These soldiers treated the Egyptian citizens like dogs, with no respect whatsoever, and ignored entirely the Egyptian officers. This insolence infuriated Farouk. He could not forget the saying, "In Egypt the only power above Allah is the British." It was this that compelled Farouk to enter into a secret agreement with Hitler that would allow Rommel to occupy the country. Hitler dispatched Joseph Goebbels to visit Farouk and work out a plan. The British, after all, had deposed Ismail the Magnificent, and not one Egyptian had raised a hand or a voice in his defense. Farouk was eager to enlist Nazi support in his desire for revenge. This, as it turned out, was not to be, and so Farouk privately vowed to find another way to expel the British. It is to his credit that British forces withdrew from Cairo and Alexandria in 1947, and evacuated Egyptian territory altogether two years later. The Moslem movement provided the force, certainly, but it was Farouk who supplied the necessary push.

Farouk had many internal enemies. The fiercest among them without question was Wahid Yusri, who also became Farida's lover. Farouk was incensed about this, even though he was madly in love at this time with the Princess Fatima Toussan, the wife of Prince Hassan Toussan, a wealthy nobleman twenty-two years her senior. The prince spent most of his time tending to his thoroughbred racehorses and so allowed Fatima ample opportunity to meet with Farouk.

Yusri and Nahas Pasha, Farouk's other archenemy, combined to make the king's political life miserable. I will never forget the February day in 1945 when the Prime Minister, Ahmed Maher Pasha, was assassinated by a young revolutionary named Mahmud el-Isawi. Farouk, who was in the process of creating the Arab League, was convinced that Yusri was behind the killing. He stormed into Farida's bedroom and vowed to cut out her vagina. Farida bore Farouk three daughters, the last of whom, also named Farida, Farouk vehemently denied having fathered. He was frustrated in his desire for a male heir, and upset that he had no blood relative to support him in his battles.

Farouk's closest friend outside the court was the former King of Albania, Ahmed Zog. Zog and Farouk met almost nightly after the war at The Scarabee, a small Cairo nightclub. It was King Zog who introduced Farouk to the actress Nadia Gray, whose real name was Princess Cantacuzino. Farouk's attempt at seducing this woman, who would become a movie star for Federico Fellini and other European directors, was a failure, and he accused Zog of poisoning her against him. Zog pointed out that it was he who had introduced Farouk to her in the first place, and berated Farouk for thinking ill of him. It was not customary for Farouk to apologize to anyone for anything he may have said or done, but he begged Zog's forgiveness for this unreasonable act. Only Zog could elicit this kind of humble behavior from Farouk.

It was Zog, too, who chided Farouk about his excesses at the gaming tables. Farouk kept a reserved seat at the *tout va*—no limit—table at the Monte Carlo casino. In Cairo he played *chemin de fer* regularly at the Royal Automobile Club on Kasr-en-Nil Street; he gambled in Cannes and Deauville; and he kept a faithful record of his losses. In one year alone Farouk lost 850,000 Egyptian pounds, at that time—1947—equivalent to 2 million American dollars. Farouk casually remarked to Zog that he, Farouk, had even gambled with the throne and won. Zog replied that one may lose many times at poker but a throne can be lost but once. Farouk then stated: "In ten years there will be only five kings left in the world. The king of clubs, the king of diamonds, the king of hearts, the king of spades, and the King of England."

Farouk divorced Farida at the same time that he forced the Shah of Iran to divorce Fawzia. Farouk hated Reza Pahlavi; he thought him personally dishonest and despised Pahlavi's father, who had previously taken asylum in South Africa. Farouk wanted no connection with the Shah. Farouk's own intention was to marry Princess Fatima but she betrayed him by marrying Prince Juan Orleans Bractara in Paris. This marriage sent Farouk into a berserk rage. He took a cane and stomped around the palace, smashing vases and furniture. He never recovered completely from this loss. Fatima was one woman he could not claim, and it galled him.

At this same time, in the late forties, Huda Sha'rawi died. She was the wife of the President of Egypt's first parliament, and in 1919 was the first woman to discard the veil. She was the leader of women's emancipation in Egypt, and strange as it may seem, Farouk revered her. It seemed to Farouk that his world was crumbling. Other than Zog, Farouk felt he could trust no one beyond his closest aides, such as Pietro, Mohammed Hassan, and me.

Farouk began spending more time on his yacht, the *Fakhr-al-Behar,* and at his house on the east bank of the Nile at Helwan, a cozy place named Roken el-Farouk ("Farouk's little corner") at which he kept rendezvous with women. He developed a taste for hashish mixed with honey, and was often unavailable for official duties for two or three days at a time. Farouk joked that the only palace he belonged in was the "yellow palace," which in Egypt is a name for the insane asylum.

Then Farouk met and married Narriman Sadek, who in 1951, the year of their marriage, was sixteen years old. She bore him his only son, Prince Said, and though their marriage was no more satisfactory in other ways than Farouk's union with Farida, he remained beholden to Narriman for having produced Said. Farouk announced to me on the night of Said's birth that he could now die happily, knowing he had earned the respect of his ancestors, particularly Ismail.

Farouk's weight continued to rise, and his preoccupations with gambling, women, and drugs increased in intensity. Pietro della Valle and I feared for his sanity, and one evening in 1951 he declared us Egyptian citizens, despite our having been born in

Italy. Being Catholic, neither of us had been circumcised as Moslem boys are at the age of thirteen. Farouk demanded that we be circumcised, though both of us were almost forty. We were forced by Farouk to undergo this extremely painful ceremony, and it was after this that I began to distance myself from him.

Farouk created a Black Brigade *à la* the Swiss Guards; Sudanese soldiers, each of whom was over six feet tall, were enlisted as a personal bodyguard. He felt endangered by the Moslem Brotherhood, an organization that wanted Egypt to declare war on England. Riots broke out in all of the cities. The Black Brigade was soon disbanded due to outbreaks among them of syphilis and other diseases. Farouk complained to me again and again that he was friendless and unloved, and I could not contradict him.

On July 26, 1952, the day Farouk abdicated the throne and he and Narriman boarded the *Mahroussa* in Alexandria to sail for Capri, I was arrested. I never saw Farouk again. I know that he at first took up residence at the Eden Paradise Hotel in Anacapri, commanding forty rooms in which to house his entourage. Farouk next ensconced himself at Frascati, south of Rome, and later, after Narriman left him and resettled with Said in Lausanne, he moved into Rome. It was there that Farouk made the acquaintance of the gangster Lucky Luciano, also in exile, who informed Farouk that there was a price on my former master's head of £140,000. Farouk knew there were many men—and probably women, too—who would gladly have him assassinated, so he never went anyplace thereafter without his Albanian bodyguards.

The end was sordid, of course. Farouk weighed more than twenty-three stone, 320 pounds. He gambled heavily, as always. Pietro remained with him and informed me later that Farouk carried a black 6.35-caliber Beretta automatic, along with pills for kidney problems and high blood pressure. I can remember when he was forced to undergo an operation for hemorrhoids; it was so painful that afterward he made Zog promise to have the doctor killed. Farouk's sexual appetite in his last years, according to Pietro, was for overweight women with large breasts and wide hips. Heavyset call girls flocked to Rome and Monte Carlo in the hope of becoming one of his favorites. I recall Farouk saying often that only a woman's ankles determined whether or not she was beautiful.

Pietro said that Farouk died of heart failure after devouring his third dinner of an evening, this last having included seven chickens, a candied ham, a dozen baked potatoes, a pot of rice, several chocolate éclairs, a Sacher torte, some kind of flaming dessert, two bottles of wine, and many cups of expresso. He had just lit one of his custom-wrapped Havana cigars, a Monte Cristo, I'm sure, when he keeled over and banged his head on the table. Farouk's last words, uttered to a prostitute he had hired for the night, were, "When the cow falls, a thousand knives appear." This is an old Egyptian proverb meaning he had no real friends, and no one to defend his memory after his death. Farouk was forty-five years old.

Salemm' Aleikoum.

A FAIR PRICE

Felice Vano knew he was not really a very good actor but he was not a bad one, either. If he were too good he would not have become a television star in Italy. Ordinary people, the ones who watched the kinds of programs Felice was featured in, identified with him more easily than they would, say, an actor of Laurence Olivier's caliber. Watching Olivier the viewer was aware a *performance* was taking place; with Felice Vano the audience—and Vano, as well—understood always that he was merely one of them, pretending to be someone he or they were not and never could be.

Vano thought about his career as he sipped an espresso and looked around at the faces in the bar. Felice liked coming home to Castel Agnese every few months. He especially enjoyed fleeing Rome during October, when the social season was raging. Felice had never cared for parties other than as a necessary evil to endure for the purpose of meeting women. At the moment he didn't care if he ever had a girlfriend again, let alone a wife, of which he had had three. This was not a fact he was proud of, especially since he would not be thirty-four years old for two more months.

Actors, Felice Vano believed, were perhaps the least well-equipped human beings on the planet to lead successful personal lives. They were forever moving around and—even if they were lucky enough to be working at the moment—hustling up their next job. Actors never had the time to find out who they really were. Felice's friend Marcello Ghezzi, who also had been an actor before committing suicide at the age of thirty, six years ago, used to say that every actor should have tattooed on one of his arms the letters *IC*, for Identity Crisis.

Vano was one of the few among his youthful contemporaries to escape Castel Agnese and its environs. Most of his childhood friends and acquaintances still lived in or around the town and worked in the agricultural industry or services related to the local tourist trade. Castel Agnese was famous for its olive groves and holiday resorts, attracting during the good weather months vacationers from all over the world. Felice's father, now in his early sixties, operated a tobacco shop in the central district assisted by his wife. Felice's mother had during her lifetime never traveled out of the region, and her husband only once, when Felice was taken at the age of sixteen to Brindisi to attend the funeral of his father's favorite aunt.

Many times Felice Vano had invited his parents, other relatives, and various friends from Castel Agnese to visit him in Rome, but nobody did. All appreciated his offer but even the thought of confronting such a potentially confusing place disconcerted them. Interestingly enough, the very few of Vano's pals who left

Castel Agnese did not stop at Rome, or not for very long, anyway. They kept going and were now living in Spain, England, the United States, Australia, and Argentina.

Felice had by chance run into Paolo Palantonio, with whom he had gone through school from the age of five to seventeen, in Los Angeles a couple of years before. Paolo was working as a waiter in a restaurant in West Hollywood. He was gay and living with a much older man, a part-time art dealer who had spent fifteen years in prison for forgery and grand larceny. "Dominic's mother is Italian," Paolo told Felice, "from Rome. She's ninety-six years old and sells crucifixes and rosary beads from a stand near the Vatican. Dominic hasn't seen her in almost forty years, but we're planning a trip next spring. I hope she'll still be alive."

Felice paid for his coffee and was about to leave the bar when a boy handed him a folded piece of paper. Vano looked at the boy, who was about fourteen years old. The only remarkable feature about his face was a drooping left eyelid. The boy smiled at Felice, then turned and walked out of the bar. Felice unfolded the piece of paper. It was a note written by an unsteady hand:

> *We have your car. It is safe. To get it back come to the entrance to the old olive grove on the Garibaldi Road on the side of the Green City where the sun dies at ten o'clock tonight. Bring ten million lire and we will give you back your car. It's a fair price. If you don't believe this is so ask around. Ten o'clock.*

Felice ran out of the bar and down the street to where he had parked his two-month-old black BMW convertible. It was gone. He looked around frantically. He was alone on the street standing in the space where his car had been.

Ten million lire. He looked at his watch. The bank would close in fifteen minutes. He could get the ten million or notify the police. Better to get the money, he decided, then go to the cops. He started walking towards the bank. Hell, the local mafiosi probably had a deal with the police, gave them a cut from every scam. Welcome home, thought Felice. Welcome fucking home.

He took a taxi to the spot, arriving a few minutes before ten. The taxi driver asked Felice if he wanted him to wait and the actor hesitated before saying no. Felice figured he could call another taxi on his cell phone in case the car-nappers didn't show. It was only after the cabdriver had gone that Vano conjured the possibility that the thieves might just roll him for the cash and keep the car, too. "I'm really stupid," he said out loud.

"You might be stupid, but you're a hell of a good actor."

Felice Vano made a three-quarter turn to his left toward the sound of the voice. A short, burly man stood directly at the entrance to the olive grove. He was wearing a western-style fringed jacket cut close to his stocky form, a string tie drawn through a silver-plated steer head, and hand-tooled carnation-red cowboy boots. Vano's first thought upon seeing the man was to ask him what movie he thought he was in.

"You brought the money? What we asked?"

Vano nodded. "Where's my car?"

"Follow me," said the burly man, who then disappeared into the olive grove.

Felice had no choice but to follow, doing his best to keep up with the surprisingly fast-moving Pugliese cowboy. The actor tripped repeatedly during this pursuit, futilely attempting to match his guide's nimble movements. After several minutes Felice found himself in a small clearing deep inside the grove. He stopped, stood still, and attempted to regain his breath. He saw his car, on either side of which stood a man, one of whom was the cowboy.

"You see," said this man, who leaned against the driver's door of the BMW, "it's in perfect condition. Take a look for yourself."

Felice Vano moved a few steps closer, then stopped again. The moon was almost full, reflecting off the car's hood as if it were a body of calm black water. Vano saw that the men closely resembled one another and that both of them were smiling. He wondered if they were carrying guns.

"Giovanni's telling the truth," said the man who was leaning against the passenger side. "We didn't put more than ten or twelve kilometers on it."

"Did you ask him if he brought the ten million?" the second man asked the first.

"He told me he's got it."

"Put the money on the hood," the second man instructed.

Vano was suddenly seized by the thought that they intended to murder him even if he paid the ransom. He stepped forward, removed two envelopes from a pocket of his jacket and placed them on the car.

"There's five million in each one," he said.

The burly men each picked up an envelope, opened it and counted the bills. When they had completed counting they stuffed the bills back into the envelopes and folded them into their coat pockets.

"It's a fair price," said Giovanni.

"A very good price," said the second man. "We're honest here in Castel Agnese. Ask anyone in the region."

"Massimo's word is famous, said Giovanni. "When he speaks it's as if God's shepherd gathered all doubts and lies together and herded them off a cliff."

To this Felice had only one response: "Where are the keys?"

"In the ignition," said Massimo.

"Is it all right if I go now," asked Vano.

"Of course," said Giovannni.

"As you like," said Massimo. "It's your car."

Felice walked to the driver's side and Giovanni opened the door for him.

"You're really a wonderful actor," he said.

"Thanks," Felice said, and got into the car. He started it up.

Massimo leaned through the passenger-side window and said, "We're great admirers of your work here in Castel Agnese. Everyone in the town is very proud of you. What was the name of that television show you were in a couple of years ago? The one where you played a former police detective who'd been thrown off the force for being drunk on duty but who kept on solving crimes anyway."

"*Musso's Case.*"

"You were Tommy Musso," said Giovanni.

"That was the character's name."

"I mean," Giovanni said, "you really *were* Tommy Musso."

"Tommy Musso will always be you," said Massimo, "that's what Giovanni means. Nobody else could be him."

"Absolutely," said Giovanni, "the public would never accept another actor in the role. Tommy Musso is you and you're him, that's it."

"I'll go now," said Felice, "if it's all right."

"Sure, of course, go," said Massimo. "But listen, do us a favor."

Felice looked at Massimo but it was Giovanni who spoke. "How about giving us a ride?" he said.

"It's a long way back," said Massimo. "We can call a taxi on the cell but who knows how long it'll take or if he'll even come. What do you say?"

Why didn't one of them drive a second car out here? thought Felice.

"Get in," he said.

Massimo climbed in next to Vano and Giovanni got in the back.

"How do I get out of the grove?"

"That way," Massimo said, pointing a finger. "Just drive, we'll tell you where to go."

When they were on the road toward the center of Castel Agnese Giovanni leaned forward and said, "Our families are having a little party tonight, kind of a celebration, you know. I'm sure everyone would like to meet you."

"I know my wife and mother would be thrilled," said Massimo. "They're great fans of yours."

"And my great-Aunt Antonella," said Giovanni, "she's eighty-six. She thinks you're more handsome than Clark Gable was."

"Gary Cooper," said Massimo. "Antonella always says Gary Cooper."

"Both of them," Giovanni said, "nothing compared to Felice Vano."

"Felice," said Massimo, "you've got to come in for a moment, just to be kind to these ladies, to be polite."

Felice flinched. "Polite?"

"The world being the way it is," said Massimo, "they might not have the opportunity again."

"How do you see the world?" asked Felice.

"You know, unpredictable."

Felice followed the men's directions and within ten minutes had parked the car in front of a large old yellow house. Massimo and Giovanni got out on the passenger side.

"Come on," Giovanni said, "just for a moment or two. You'll be making some little people happier than you can imagine."

While driving away from the olive grove Vano had decided to drop off the men and continue straight to the police station; but now, absurd as it seemed, he knew he would accompany Massimo and Giovanni into the house.

"Did you get the money?" a woman of about sixty with a blue turban wrapped around her head asked Massimo as he came first through the door. Immediately behind him was Felice Vano, then Giovanni.

"We did, Mama. Everything went perfectly."

"He didn't go to the police?"

"No, Mama. Look, here he is, just to say hello to the family."

Massimo's mother clasped her hands against her cheeks and shouted, "It's him! It's really him! Felice Vano, the great actor, in our house!"

She grabbed one of Felice's hands and clutched it to her chest, yanking him toward her as she did so, pressing her massive breasts against his abdomen.

"Mama, be careful with the man!"

"Tell me, Signor Vano," she implored, "how much did you pay?"

By now a dozen or more people had gathered around and behind Massimo's mother. Felice looked at their curious, eager faces and wanted to run. Standing directly behind him, however, were Giovanni and Massimo.

"Ten million lire," said Felice.

"Ah! A fair price!" exclaimed Massimo's mother. Her wide, square face was contorted into a smile that resembled a rumpled bedsheet. Felice was suddenly frightened by the thought that she was going to kiss him and swallow him in the process.

"A very fair price," repeated someone behind Massimo's mother.

Others nodded their heads as they murmured their assent. Massimo came forward and extracted Felice from his mother's python-like arms, then guided him toward a younger version of the same woman.

"This is my wife, Gabriella," said Massimo. "Gabriellina, meet Felice Vano, the best actor ever to be born in Castel Agnese."

Gabriella brushed Felice's right hand with a wet palm.

"It's a pleasure to meet you," he said.

Massimo's wife suddenly sprang up and directly at Felice's face like an Egyptian cobra, kissing him between his eyes. She drew back, shuddering. Tears streamed down her cheeks. Felice was shocked, mystified, and horrified all at the same time. Gabriella buried her head in her husband's chest.

Giovanni took Felice's left arm. "I want you to meet my great-Aunt," he said. "Remember, I told you about her."

Felice glided along in Giovanni's embrace. They stopped in front of an ancient, tiny woman who was sitting in a flat-bottomed, high-backed wooden chair. She seemed to be asleep.

"Antonella," Giovanni half-shouted, "look who's here!"

The wizened old lady opened her two enormous black eyes and stared directly into Felice's. He could hardly bear the ferocity of her gaze. Inside this atrophied body, he realized, there thrived a still-terrible beast.

"How much did they ask to get back the car?" crowed Antonella.

"Ten million," answered Felice.

"A fair price," she said, half-closing her ferocious eyes. Antonella flashed them again for a second and croaked, "We're honest people here," before falling back to sleep.

Felice straightened and extricated himself from Giovanni's hold.

"I've got to be going," he said.

Giovanni nodded and grinned. He extended his right hand and shook Felice's.

"You're always welcome in this house."

Massimo came over.

"Felice's leaving," said Giovanni.

"Have a glass of wine," Massimo said. "Eat some salsiccia."

"No, thanks," said Felice.

Massimo grabbed Felice's hand. "Thank you for coming," he said. "It's really meant a lot to us, to all of us. If you ever need anything in Castel Agnese—anything—let us know."

Felice nodded and started for the front door but Massimo tightened his grip on the actor's hand.

"Promise you will," said Massimo.

He looked into Massimo's eyes. Antonella, Felice realized, was Massimo's grandmother.

"I will," he said.

THE OLD DAYS

Felix Martucci took his time getting off the plane. He had to because of the instability of his left knee, which had been replaced three months before, but he also enjoyed the feeling, the luxury of moving leisurely and the general latitude given by others to a person of a certain age. Felix Martucci would be eighty-four years old in six weeks, a fact that he found difficult to entirely comprehend. Each morning when he looked at his face in the mirror he asked himself, "Who is that guy?"

Martucci had never been indolent, nor had he been a nervous type. His calm but purposeful demeanor was always a plus. Men trusted him, and in his business—or what formerly had been his business—this was the finest attribute of all. To be feared was not without benefits, but trust, as Benny Pickles put it, was the grandfather of respect. Benny Pickles, poor man, may he rest in peace. Gone now how many years? Five? Six? Everybody was gone, just about, except himself. Whoever else was still alive wasn't worth a thought.

Felix stepped carefully to the exit and paused briefly, closing his eyes before emerging onto the platform of the stairway. He took a deep breath and opened his eyes, looking out at Havana for the first time in forty years. Strange, he thought, not to have a strong feeling of any kind at this moment. The air was sultry but not quite as warm as he had expected it to be. A flight steward took his arm, a young man. Felix sized him up.

"May I be of assistance, sir? The stairs are a little wet."

In the old days, thought Felix, it would have been a pretty young woman holding his elbow. This guy was probably a fag, but what the hell. Junie's boy, Marty, was a fag, and he was a pretty good kid, a good grandson. It didn't matter any more, not much did. Fuck the old days, too. He hated that expression.

Felix negotiated the stairs without slipping. He wondered if the steward knew who he was, that he'd been responsible for the premature demise of more than a few men—not that they hadn't earned their deaths—whether he would handle the elderly gentleman in such a tender fashion.

Back in the fifties, Felix recalled, there was always a car to meet him on the tarmac next to the plane, usually a late-model convertible. Today he took a taxi, a 1957 Chevy Bel Air held together by wire and spit. There had to be some marvelous automobile mechanics in Cuba, able to keep these ancient vehicles percolating.

He would stay at the Hotel Nacional, as he had always done. In Miami, Felix preferred the Biltmore, in the Gables. Both hotels had been designed by the same man. People knew what style and elegance were back then. Just look at Vegas to see what things have come to, if you can do it and keep from puking. Fat parents with fat kids eating ice cream cones, all of them wearing shorts. Casinos in shopping malls with animal acts, for God's sake.

Felix Martucci sat on the terrace smoking a Cohiba, the only thing he could thank Castro for creating. Felix didn't know if the one he was smoking was the real goods or not, but it tasted. Since his second heart attack he hadn't touched tobacco or alcohol. Now he sipped a mojito and puffed away. It wouldn't be so terrible, he figured, to die in this place, a city filled with good memories for him. The government here had finally wised up and started behaving like the Syndicate. Plenty of new hotels and cheap hookers were bringing in the suckers, mostly from Europe and Canada, of course, but those people could spend too.

Once at the Riviera with Lipsky a made guy out of Cleveland named Nicky Pants tried to cut a deal for the docking charges. Lipsky wanted to know what he had to offer and Nicky Pants said the casino boat on Lake Erie. There wasn't any casino boat on Lake Erie. What was he talking about? Lipsky could put one there and this Nicky Pants would keep it safe. Lipsky didn't know how an escaped mental patient got in the room. Nicky Pants raised his voice. The next morning he was found tied to a piling, his legs bitten to the bone by barracudas. Felix had been happy to do a service for Lipsky. The man made everything go in Havana and Martucci went with it.

The water still looked pretty good. There didn't used to be so many young people hanging around on the streets. At least he didn't think so. What a shame the place had to go to the dogs, a real waste. It wasn't just the real estate, either; it was the people. They liked a good time. Felix smiled at the memory of watching a golden-skinned woman with big black eyes wearing only a live snake while she danced at the Tropicana. The snake's head rested on her left breast, its tongue flicking out and in in time to the music, its only moving part. Now that was an act. Maybe in Asia it's done, but back then, only in Cuba.

There was another reason Felix Martucci had come to Havana, one aside from nostalgia. He had a son here. The boy, if he was alive, would be forty-two years old. Not a boy anymore. The same age Felix was when he was born. His name was Felix, too; at least it had been the last time he'd seen him. Little Felix was two then, a coffee-colored kid with wild, wavy black hair like his father had when he was young. Where his son's mother was now Martucci had no clue. She might be dead, of course. Her name was Sonya Despacio, and she'd been twenty-four when they'd met, a dancer at the Hi-Hat, one of Benedetti's clubs.

Martucci had rarely thought about this son over the years. He had enjoyed a decent enough if not terribly close relationship with his three daughters and six grandchildren. Until she died a year ago, Anna's life revolved around the kids and their lives. Felix pretty much stayed out of the fray. Since Anna's passing after fifty-one years of marriage, Felix had stayed mostly to himself, content to allow the housekeeper prepare meals and answer the telephone. He watched ball games, read mystery novels, and played cards once or twice a week with the few cronies he had left.

The thought to visit Havana and the remote possibility of finding Little Felix energized him. But now that he was here, Martucci really wasn't sure what to do. Getting to Cuba had been simple: He flew to Cancun, Mexico, and from there to

Havana. Nobody blinked an eye at the several Americans, including himself, making the trip despite the United States government's prohibition on travel to the island. Felix just made certain his passport wasn't stamped, though he couldn't have cared less about getting into trouble. What could anybody, even the government, do to an octogenarian who'd had two heart attacks in the past two years?

Sonya was engaged to be married when Felix met her. They spent a week together at Varadero Beach in a villa Lipsky kept there. She was dark-skinned except for light patches under her arms and behind her knees. At certain moments parts of her looked almost blue, especially after she'd been in the sun for an extended period of time. Felix told her she reminded him of some exotic tropical fish. Sonya's brown eyes had bright yellow flames in them that appeared to leap out when she became particularly excited. Felix described them once as two flares igniting simultaneously, penetrating his soul in a way nobody else ever had. He knew Sonya had never loved him, and Felix was not sure he had ever loved her. Nevertheless, he attached a significance to their relationship that was unique in his experience.

Oddly enough for Felix Martucci, he felt a certain amount of guilt for having virtually abandoned Sonya Despacio and their son. He had not been a man to feel much guilt about anything. He gave money to Sonya every time he was in Havana over a period of two years. After he stopped coming, he contributed nothing to her and Little Felix's welfare.

What could he do now to make up for this? Even if he located Sonya and Felix, Jr., he could not imagine that their response to him would be at all positive. He was an American gangster on his last legs—leg, actually—an enemy of the regime they had been living under and probably brainwashed by for the majority of their lives. Felix, Jr., of course, had never known any other way of life. The possibility did exist, Martucci realized, that she and the boy might have fled the island during the Mariel boatlift in 1981, or by some other means at another time. They could even be living in the United States right now.

A jet passed overhead, leaving in its wake a vapor trail a half-mile long that resembled a herd of elephants dispersing in several directions. Felix sipped his mojito, the first alcoholic drink he'd had in more than a year. He was reminded of the time Milwaukee Dave Indennizzare shot and killed a policeman in a whorehouse in the old section of Havana. The cop had gotten upset that Dave had taken his regular girl at the hour customarily reserved for him. There was an argument and the cop pulled his gun first. Dave had a drink in his hand, which he tossed the contents of into the cop's face. The cop never fired a shot, but Dave got his piece out and nailed the cop. After the body had been removed from the premises, Dave asked for a fresh mojito to replace the one he'd wasted. When Lipsky heard the story he said from that time on Indennizzare should be called Mojito Dave.

Martucci hated thinking that his life was over, that there was no way to get it back, to have more time. He'd heard Walt Disney's head had been severed from its body and been preserved cryogenically in the hope that one day medical science would be able to reactivate his brain. Felix didn't want that—he just wanted to have a few more years as he was. It didn't look promising. Fuck complaining. Complaining was for the new generation. Those guys, all they knew how to do good was beef. Beef and betray each other. That's why this whole thing was over. Assimilation had done it. Blood meant nothing if it was thinned down too much.

Two more jet fighters flew over. Maybe on their way to or from Guantanamo, though the airspace directly over Havana, Felix thought, would have been severely restricted. Who knows what kinds of deals these politicians got.

A waiter came out onto the terrace and asked Felix if he wanted another drink. The waiter looked to be about forty years old.

"*¿Como se llama?*" Felix asked him.

"Benicio."

Martucci nodded and handed his almost empty glass to Benicio. "*¿Porqué no?*"

The waiter placed the glass on a small tray and walked away. What if he'd said his name was Felix? What if he were the son of an old bad guy? What difference would it really make to anyone?

The sky clouded over. Felix reached down with his right hand and felt his cock through his trousers. He probably had prostate cancer, too, along with the heart condition. He'd read that eighty-five percent of all men eventually get cancer of the prostate, though most of them die of another ailment. Prostate cancer usually advanced slowly. He knew guys who'd had their prostates removed, surgery that left them impotent or incontinent or both. Better at this age just to let it go. At least he could still raise a hard-on now and again.

Benicio showed up with the mojito.

"Will there be anything else, sir," he asked in perfect English.

"Do you know a man in his early forties, looks a little like you, named Felix? Felix Despacio. His mother's name is Sonya."

"No, I don't believe so."

"Okay, then. Thanks."

Felix watched the waiter walk away, then he closed his eyes, resting the glass containing the rum concoction on his chest. He could hear the jets.

BARRY GIFFORD'S novels have been translated into twenty languages. His book *Night People* was awarded the Premio Brancati in Italy, and he has been the recipient of awards from PEN, the National Endowment for the Arts, and the American Library Association. David Lynch's film based on Gifford's novel *Wild at Heart* won the Palme d'Or at the Cannes Film Festival in 1990, and Barry Gifford's novel *Perdita Durango* was made into a feature film in 1997. Barry Gifford co-wrote with director David Lynch the film *Lost Highway*, also released in 1997. Mr. Gifford's most recent books include *The Phantom Father: A Memoir* (named a *New York Times* Notable Book of the Year); and *Wyoming*, a novel, which has been adapted for the stage, and is soon to be a major motion picture.